MW00510820

THE LEGEND OF AVLVS

FLORA·MACDONALD·SHEARER

WILLIAM DOXEY
·:SAN FRANCISCO:·
M:D:CCC:XC:VI

CONTENTS.

CONTENTS.

BALLADES, SONNETS, AND OTHER VERSES—

NOTE.

The original sketch of "The Legend of Aulus" may be found in the "Gesta Romanorum."

THE LEGEND OF AULUS.

I.

Hidden amid the Apennines, there lies
A lake unfathomable, deep-shelving, dark.
Strange stories cling about the place, and fill
The very air with mystery and dread;
And often, when on long black winter nights
The peasant tells them to his huddling brood,
The children shudder at the shadows cast
By the unsteady firelight on the wall,
The women drop their spinning in affright,
And cross themselves and call on all the saints.

I, lingering late among these barren hills,
Saw such a scene and heard this story told:

Centuries since a law was made in Rome,
Enacting that no citizen should wed
The maiden of his choice unless he stood
Prepared to dower her with gold or lands
Of value equal to her own estate.
An evil law it was, but so enforced,
So straitly bound by form and precedent,
That none, or few, its harsh requirements broke;
Sorrow it wrought and bitterness extreme.

In those dim days upon the Aventine Mount
An ancient mansion reared its noble front;
Built of the famous marble which endures
The slow-corroding years, the earthquake shock,
Its white walls gleamed beneath the fervid sky,
Towering in grandeur o'er the roofs of Rome.

One autumn eve upon its battlements
A lady leaned and watched the sun's decline,
Nor watched alone, for by her stood a knight,

Equipped as for the field, in mail complete;
A soldier he of the Prætorian Guard,
And near the person of the Emperor,
But landless, with no fortune save his sword.

Long time they stood and marked the increas-
    ing night
Shadow the hills and darken o'er the plain,
But little said, until the stars awoke,
And in the sky their feeble lanterns lit;
When, downward looking on her face, the knight
Saw tears thereon, which, furtive, she concealed,
And sudden cried, "What, my Faveria, tears,—
Tears on this night—and I so new returned,
And after so long absence?—but, perchance,
By these disparted years thy faith is strained
Nigh even to breaking, and thy heart, I fear,
Is now to one more fortunate resigned.
If this be so——" "Nay, Aulus, all my care
Is only thee to please and thee to love,

And, for these foolish drops, dismiss them quite,
Or think them but a moment's fantasy,
A passing whim, for often women weep."

"Pardon, Faveria, pardon these my words,
Hasty and choleric as my nature is;
To lose you death, far worse your faith to
 doubt,—
For jealous doubt is a tormenting fire
Which eats the heart. Of this no more—and
 now,
I prithee let me wipe the traitor stains
That cloud the brightness of these dearest eyes,
My lode-stars through the desert of this world.
Yet, in good sooth, it passeth all belief
That you, who are so young, exceeding fair,
Of so great name, and all too richly dowered
Should ever sigh or waste a weary hour."

"Little it profits to be rich and fair;
My wealth it is betwixt us two that stands,

And for my fairness—Dido's face was fair,
Yet could she not Æneas long retain.
Beauty in woman is an April day,
Mere streaks of sunshine through the clouds
    that rift;
In youth adored, when time our charm hath
    marred,
Slight is the homage to our virtues paid.
In heat of battle men their cares forget,
Or on the Forum, or in council grave,
But women sit alone within the house,
And idly o'er the inevitable brood.
We smile upon the splendor of the rose,
Nor see the canker in its heart that grows."

Then Aulus: "Much, Faveria, have I dwelt
On this, our mutual unhappy strait,
And in the night when all my comrades slept,
Have I, uneasy, paced the camp about,
Nor found an answer to my questioning,

Save one,—but no, this black, accursed deed
Be far from me——"

         "Nay, Aulus, voice thy thought;
What thou canst bear to think, thy lips can
    speak."

And answer made the knight in broken words:
"A new decree the Emperor hath passed—
Thereof thou art informed?"

             "Of such a law
A rumor vague and unconfirmed is all
The talk of Rome."

        "Then know that Constantine
Disbanded hath the old Prætorian Guard.
Our cohorts, through the empire all dispersed,
By this disunion lose their primal strength,
And to the throne cease to be dangerous.
This edict yet more closely sets the bars
Which now asunder hold us. There remains
One way, and one alone, whereby our hands

Forever may be joined——"

       "Aulus, my lord,
Make swift thy speech till all thy tale be told."

"Far to the northward in the Apennines,
Dwelleth Hortensius, my next of kin;
Great is his wealth,—yea, greater than thine
  own.
Blind from his birth, in solitude he lives,
The castle scantly guarded.   All the place
To me is known, for oft its hollow courts
Have I with boyish laughter heedless filled,
And with the step of active youth explored
Each crumbling stair and dim, remote recess.
Thither 'tis in my purpose to repair,
And secret in the night his soul dispatch,
My horse regain and rapid spur to Rome,
All unsuspect——"

      "A murder! hear, ye gods!
To take his life who naught hath injured thee,

Nor in fair fight, but while he helpless lies —
O most intolerable and bloody thought! —
My curses on the hand that framed this law!"

"Then fare-thee-well, Faveria; here and now
Dear is thy love; thine honor so more dear
That never shall the slime of slander trail
Across its sacred whiteness, and if death
Do claim me on the field,—right welcome he."

"To-night we part?——"

                              "I go this very hour."
"And thou canst leave me lonely in this world —
Alone I am; in blankness stretch the years
Where thou art not; but — hold, were this man
      dead
To part no need?"

                        "I wait upon thy word."
"Together we might live, together share
The round of life, its common bliss and pain;

The coming death together we might meet,
Smile at his harmless shaft and know content.
Enough — 'tis ended; count the deed as done.
To rush us to our doom the Fates conspire.
But be thou merciful; make sure thy hand,
And give his soul a speedy taking-off."

"Thou speakest to the tenor of my will,
And now my purpose is determinate.
But look, beloved, how the conquering day
Against the blackness of the night prevails;
I must be gone, and swiftly, nor do thou
With o'er much thinking knit the troubled
    brow."

He spoke and passed; she, backward gazing
    there,
A moveless, breathless statue of despair.

II.

The birds their waking music trilled,
The sky with early light was filled,
As Aulus seized his horse's rein
And vaulted to his seat again.
The sleeping streets, as on he sped,
Echoed beneath his horse's tread.
A moment on the bank he stood
Where sacred Tiber pours his flood,
Then past the hill Capitoline,—
Once of Tarpeian Jove the shrine,—
And by the old Nomentane Way,
He reached the camp at height of day,
And saw the Labarum unfold
Its veil of purple and of gold.

The troops by the Prætorium
Are massed, and slow the Augurs come,
Portentous, grave, and knowing well
By signs the future to foretell.

Eager they scan the devious flight
Of birds uncertain.   To the right
They circling wheel — propitious sign, —
The gods appeased on mortals shine.
The soldiers cheer; dismissed, they pass
The idle hour with song and glass.
But Aulus to the tribune's tent
Hasted, and gained his chief's consent
To furlough brief; and ere the day
Had glided o'er the hills away,
Beneath the ancient gate he strode,
Which guards the great Flaminian road.
Swift was his courser's pace; he passed
Pons Milvius, and saw at last
Between him and the evening sky
The desolate Campagna lie.

For five long days he onward took
His lonely way, with scarce a look
On hill, or wood, or castled mound.
Yet where could fairer scenes be found?

For royal Tiber, rolling free
His murky waters to the sea,
Companioned him for mile on mile,
By vale, and cliff, and dark defile;
And oaks, with leaves of evergreen,
About his pathway wove their screen;
Where groves of box and alder were,
The clematis its glory there
Now careless trailed upon the ground,
Now massed some hoary trunk around;
The broom a passing perfume lent
To each faint breeze that wandering went,
And, over all, the burning blue
Of heaven its airy archway threw.

At Interamna short his stay;
Leaving the broad Flaminian Way,
He rode beneath the scented pines
That skirt the lower Apennines,
And sought a bridle track that led
Beside a mountain torrent's bed.

So difficult the steep ascent,
He reached the top with forces spent,
And flung him on the mosses brown,
And heard the water foaming down.
But night was closing o'er the scene,
And hill and valley stretched between,
Although but half a league away
The dwelling of his fathers lay.
Beneath a tree he tied his horse,
And wearily pursued his course.
At first the path he scarce could find,
With brier and bramble intertwined;
The sky with clouds was overspread,
Chill blew the wind about his head;
The thunder crashed, the tempest lowered,
And from the lightning flash he cowered.

Upon a cliff the castle stood,
Fit to defy the storm and flood.
　High on the rugged height

Its walls arose, the dwelling-place
For ages of a warrior race
Who drank of battle and the chase
　　The keen and wild delight.
Their ashes in sepulchral urns,
　　Drenched with the wine of death,
Regardless lie; before them burns
　　The taper's flickering breath.
Small heed have they of praise or blame,
Forgot their glory and their shame.

A lamp within a window gleamed,
Its radiance through the darkness streamed;
　　There sat Hortensius.
Shut from the friendly light, he dwelt
In visionary lands, and dealt
In lore occult, the nearness felt
　　Of forms unseen by us

Who know the splendor of the world,—
  The mountain in its dignity,
With wreaths of mist about it curled,
  And the far-reaching sea.
Bravely he bore his banishment;
In dreams he lived, with dreams content.

As Aulus watched the lighted tower,
And waited for the midnight hour,
  His thoughts were dark to tell.
These silent halls had many a day
Resounded with their youthful play;
The children of two brothers, they
  Had loved each other well,
Ere years came with resistless change.
  One wandered o'er the earth,
The other never cared to range
  Far from his place of birth;
But each remembered in his prime
The innocent glad morning-time.

Aulus was lost to time and place,
When, sudden showering on his face,
He felt the heavy raindrops fall,
And sought the shelter of the wall.
With stealthy search a door he gained
By clustering ivy hid, unchained
The rusted hasp, and passed to where
He might attain the secret stair
That to the turret led where slept
Hortensius. As soft he crept,
He started back at every sound
Made on the stairway's crumbling round.

And now he stands within the room,
But vainly strives to pierce the gloom,
Till, by the lightning's fitful aid,
He sees the couch whereon is laid
Hortensius in slumber deep,
Unguarded in the castle keep.
His head is pillowed on his arm,
In vain security from harm,

And some fair thought his dream beguiles;
He sleeps, and as he sleeps he smiles.

With steady stroke the deed was done.
One sobbing moan he gave—but one,—
A feeble cry, on earth unheard,
But angels caught the parting word,—
For to the knight's astonished sight,
On shining feather, winged its flight
A bird that perched upon the bed,
And nestled near the dead man's head.
Strange visitant in so dread place,
And in such hour!   A moment's space
It rested there; then, uttering
A sweet, strange note, it plumed its wing;
Back to the night and dismal rain
It passed, and ne'er was seen again.

Forth from the castle fled the knight,
Nor slacked his speed till morning light.

Madly he rode to ease the pain
That ached about his heart — in vain.
The mountain peaks grew far and dim,
But guilt and fear kept pace with him.
He grudged the time for rest or food,
Till safe within the camp he stood;
The curtains of his tent he drew,
And soon in sleep oblivion knew.

Upon the palace roof once more
The two are met; not as before
Hand clasped in hand.   Ah, piteous change!
Guilt and remorse their hearts estrange.
But love despiseth fear and shame,
And to his side Faveria came,
And softly called him by his name.
Aulus upraised his drooping head,
And gently to Faveria said,
"Three heavy weeks have o'er us rolled —
Would that their tale had ne'er been told!

Of all that passed I may not speak
To dim your eye and blanch your cheek.
I sent you by a trusty hand
A message you could understand,
And you alone.   Hortensius hath
By me been slain, and now the path
To you and love is clear; but know
Could I the deed retract, the blow
Had ne'er been struck.   In battle's rage,
When men their country's foes engage,
With furious thrust in equal fight,
Even then death is a woeful sight.
How past all pardon is my guilt,
A friend's—a kinsman's—blood I've spilt!
My caitiff sword within his heart
I plunged—a demon winged the dart—
A painless death and swift he died.
'T were well with me if by his side
This night I lay, wrapped in the mould,
As still, as lifeless, and as cold!

And now outside the walls of Rome,
Beneath Saint Paulus' lofty dome,
His body rests.   I followed it
With needful rites, observance fit;
And, as the nearest of his kin,
Beheld it placed the tomb within.
Slowly the passing bell was tolled,
The mounting music heavenward rolled;
In rapturous, triumphant song,
It swept the sounding nave along;
Its joyous descant seemed to me
Of lasting life the prophecy;
And yet—What dost thou think of death?
Where speeds the soul with parting breath?
Can spirits from the leaden urn
Or from the inclasping grave return?"

"Countless the vague traditions be,
All touched with doubt and mystery,
   And held by some as fabulous,

Which seem to show that all the tale
Is not yet told when still and pale
   We lie, and friends make moan for us.
Shadows impalpable may pass
Through gates of iron or of brass—
But wherefore dost thou question thus?"

"A legend of our Christian faith
There is; or false, or true, it saith
   That upon All Souls' eve,
Which at to-morrow's twilight falls,
The dead forsake their sombre halls,
   The grave's embraces leave;
And on the earth, or in the air,
They wait attentive to the prayer
   Made for their souls' repose
By holy monks in church or cell.
This was my thought:—Were it not well
   That at the evening's close
I to the chapel should repair,

To spend the night in vigil there,
   And all that I may learn
To thee at dawn with speed relate?—
Thereby, perchance, the will of fate
   We clearer may discern."

"Go thou and watch the night away,
And I to all the gods will pray
   For thy desired return.
And, now, farewell, for needful sleep
Thy body craves, this watch to keep."
   Aulus upon her face,
Which shone as fair as spirits shine,
Long looked, to grave its every line
Upon his heart; then, with brief sign
   Of parting, left the place.
Alone upon the palace roof,
She heard his horse's clattering hoof
Die down the hill, and soon the night
Was all transformed beneath the light

Of the great moon that up the sky
Swam in her billowing majesty.

III.

As Aulus neared the church, he heard the bell
  For vespers peal from the adjacent tower,
And stayed his steps, subdued beneath the
    spell,
  The soft enchaining of the evening hour.
  The dry earth, kissed to freshness by a
    shower,
Was very fair; he looked, and groaned aloud;
  For him had Nature lost her healing power;
The autumn moon, emerging from a cloud,
Seemed to his gaze a dead face gleaming from
    its shroud.

Of all the great basilicas in Rome,
  Not one more famed than this where now
    is laid

Hortensius, closed within his narrow home;
  For here St. Paul's long resting-place is
    made;
  The columned arch, the altar dim-arrayed,
The timbered roof, and sculptured architrave,
  The past proclaim, in dignity displayed.
And now the bell hath ceased; within the nave
The people pass; with them the knight, apart
    and grave.

The final Gloria had long been sung,
  But Aulus still before the altar kneeled,
And to the priest confessed, with faltering
    tongue,
  And his intent to watch that night revealed.
  Silent the holy father heard, unsealed
The wrath of heaven, and penance dire
    imposed,
  And his assent unwillingly did yield,

Then slow the chapel left. The door was
    closed.
Alone the knight remained with those who
    there reposed.

Hour after hour fled on.   The silences
    Of night, more dreadful than its sounds,
      he heard,
And was aware of ghostly presences,
    That, flitting by, the air about him stirred.
    But no hand touched him, nor did any word
The stillness break.   His vigil grew apace.
    At midnight came a rush of wings that
      whirred
Rapid and ceased;—a light, and lo! the face
Of dead Hortensius, lit by a resplendent grace.

A lucent angel held him by the hand,
    And to the trembling knight these words
      addrest:

"Hear thou the will of God, by whose com-
  mand
  Have I this night to Hades passed, to wrest
  This soul from its confines, and with the
  blest
On high to seat him.   Now his joys begin.
  Thy doom attend;— by the Divine behest
To thee are granted thrice ten years wherein
His pardon thou mayst seek who can forgive
  thy sin."

Swift as a flash of light, the twain were gone,
  And Aulus gazed into the gloom profound,
And cast himself the marble floor upon,
  And prayed for death, and sank into a
  swound.
  Him thus the priest at early morning found,
And with his cares revived.   Free from that
  hall,
  How pure the dawn, what music in each
  sound!

He was as one escaping from a pall.
Straight to Faveria he passed, and told her all.

IV.

Upon her white hand leaning her gold head,
The tale Faveria heard, then, soft, she said:

"Aulus, my lord, no man upon this earth
Of his own will had e'er been brought to birth;
For who would choose some doubtful years to
    live
Where pain abides and joy is fugitive?
Great are our sorrows, and our pleasures small;
Nor know we when the fatal stroke may fall;
The very trees have longer date than we,
The birds more happy, and the beasts more free;
And when Mercurius shuts the door on us,
And on our white lips lies the obolus,
The scene is closed, nor can we surely know
If to Elysium or the Shades we go.

But the high gods have given to mortals love,
With all the bitter and the sweet thereof;
Therefore I do accept these thirty years,
And, since I love thee, banish idle fears.
Here is my hand, I pledge thee fealty —
Yea, by the head of Jove, I swear to thee."

Low bent the knight and kissed his lady's hand,
With whispered words that lovers understand,
And silence was between them for a space,
Until Faveria looking on his face
Beheld it troubled. "Why so sad, my lord?"
She murmured with caressing in each word.
"Not sad, Faveria," replied the knight,
"When you are by me sadness taketh flight;
But when I pass beyond your beauty's sway,
I dread the night and fear the coming day,
For I believe (such is the Christian creed)
That vengeance follows on an evil deed.

A heavy penance yet remains to dree
Ere from the stain of blood this hand is free;
E'en then most hardly I my soul shall save,
And terror shrouds the gulf beyond the grave."

Abrupt he paused,—Faveria answered low,
"Of this new worship little do I know,
For I in early youth to Gaul was sent,
Whither my father with his legion went;
In secret there he kept the ancient faith,
And vowed me to it with his latest breath.
But for this Christus whom you tell me of
With his strange emblems of the fish and dove,
If he, indeed, his majesty resigned,
And suffered on the cross for all mankind,
And bent his back beneath the scourger's rod,
Bethink thee—he must be a gentle god.
Make thou lustration due before his shrine,
Consult the omens and thy fate divine."

"A useless task, for no such sacrifice,"
Said Aulus, "may find favor in his eyes;
He asks alone a pure and contrite heart,
And wills that men from evil shall depart;
For he who highest heaven would hope to win
Must purge his conscience and abjure his sin.
But all these matters are for you too deep,—
Your eyes are heavy,—go, my love, and sleep.
Since you are willing o'er this heart to reign,
These shadows shall not long disturb my brain.
Perish the past—a new life hath begun—
Our faiths may differ but our hearts are one.
This night I go the castle to prepare,
Ne'er 'neath its lintel borne, a bride so fair."

Ere the next silver moon its light had shed,
All was accomplished and the twain were wed.

V.

With light the castle shines; its windows blaze
Like jewels, in the dark.   A festal night
Is this when Aulus welcomes back his son
From distant wars.   Where'er the eagle flew
His steps had followed.   Now in triumph come
The legions home.   Janus his gates hath closed;
Peace rules the Roman world; the peoples rest.

In the triclinium the feast is spread,
Whose floor of rich mosaic fitly blent
Upholds the ivory couches gold inlaid,
Or curious carven of the tortoise shell.
The men recline; graceful the women lean
On silken pillows soft as woven wind.
The dice are cast and Lucius wins the throw,
And to the seat of honor Aulus leads
His only son; well pleased the mother smiles.
Now slaves approach laden with dewy crowns
Of freshest roses; these the guests adjust;

A distant music sounds, the feast begins,
And all is laughter, jest, and quick reply.

Upon Faveria's brow a shadow lies;
Frequent her smile and seeming gay her mien,—
But seeming only, for 't is All-Souls' Eve,
And thirty years have noiseless winged away,
Too happy to be noted in their flight.
Now she remembers slain Hortensius,
The midnight vigil and the angel's words,
Veiled, yet foreshadowing mysterious woe;
And vaguely fears yet knows not what she
        fears.
For Aulus, while resisting all her wiles
To win him back unto the ancient faith,
Is to his own become indifferent.
The mass he still attends, and due observes
All customary rites, but penitence
And prayer are little in his thought or deed.
With careful glance her husband's face she eyes;

No gloom is there; among his guests he moves,
A courteous host, a chivalrous, proud knight,
And all her heart goes out to him in love,
And she is glad that he remembers not.

And now the wine is poured.   The guests
        arise
And drink in silence; to the Thunderer first,
And then to all the gods, and to the shades
Of heroes dear to every Roman heart;
And toast succeeds to toast and songs are
        heard
In sweet accord with the low-breathing lute,
When one, more near to Lucius than the rest,
His chosen friend and comrade in the wars,
Thus cries, "My Lucius, do you still retain
The careless measures of the song you made
In Africa?   Right jocund did it ring
Around our camp-fire in the starry night."
And Lucius at his bidding merry sings:

Ho, brothers, while we 're marching
   Throughout the dusty day,
With black clouds over-arching,
   And danger by the way,
Wine makes our spirit light,
And cheers us for the fight;
   Then pass the flagon gaily,
   And sing this anthem daily,
Hail to the gods, all gods above,
The noble gods of wine and love!

The night mists round us hover,
   There 's wailing in the wind —
The amphoras uncover,
   The maid we love is kind;
And since life may not last,
We make it no long fast,
   But pass the flagon gaily,
   And sing this anthem daily,
Hail to the gods, all gods above,
The noble gods of wine and love!

With joyous palm the laughing guests applaud;
The mother a reproving finger shakes,
And gently speaks, "My Lucius, for the camp
Thy strain is fit, but strange in ladies' ears.
Give now command that the musicians play
The little simple song I used to sing
Over thy cradle in the years agone;
Thy father made it in an earlier day."
And Lucius waves his hand, the harps prelude
Upon their silver strings and voices rise:

O, love is beautiful ere he grows old,
   Full of surprises, gentle and kind!
Feathery ashes, a hearth that is cold,
   Stript of disguises, fools, fools and blind!
     Eheu fugaces,
      Old love, adieu!
     Time as it passes
      Parts me and you.

O, love is beautiful when he grows old,
  Tried by distresses, tender, divine,
Stronger than iron and purer than gold,
  Our life he blesses, your life and mine.
      Eheu fugaces,
        Say not adieu!
      Time as it passes
        Binds me and you.

The night wears onward to the turning hour.
A sudden storm bears downward from the north;
Around the house in frantic glee it sweeps,
But by the merry throng is scarce remarked.
Intent some watch the fortunes of the dice,
And other some along the level board
The balls of sparkling agate whirling send.
At last the players from their curtained seat
Intone the solemn movement of a hymn,
Austere and sad, befitting well the theme,
But in so gay concourse, all unexpect.

Ye direful Fates! Creatures of death and doom!
  Let me no longer plead to you in vain.
Reverse the busy, ever-turning loom,
  Wherein is spun my life's entangled skein.

Weave but a thread of silver in the woof,
  And leave the warp all dark as now it is,
Then shall I praise you, and for your behoof
  Bring golden gifts, disastrous deities.

Implacable! the dreary voices moan
  Low, dreadful words of horror and despair:
Thy fate is fixed, forth shalt thou fare alone,
  A viewless ghost upon the wandering air.

Scarcely have died away the closing chords
When through the open casement flies a bird
Of silken plumage, brown with flecks of gold,
And on the breast and wings a purple dye.
Dazed by the storm, it circles round the hall,

With never-ceasing cry, unearthly sweet,
But sorrowful beyond all human speech.
And Aulus sees and knows the bird of fate,
For close beside him stands Hortensius,
Invisible to all save only him.
No darkness on his brow, no wrathful look,
But pardon, pity, and enduring love,
And on his lips the smile that angels wear.

Then Aulus, as a reed before the blast
Is bent and shaken, bows his head in fear
And penitence and bitter late remorse.
Clear and insistent rings the warning cry,
And summoning the rebel powers of will
An upward glance he casts — the Shade hath
        passed.
Within his own he takes Faveria's hand,
And pointing to the bird, thus to his wife
Exclaims, "All's at an end — the hour of doom
Hath struck — the messenger of ill, behold!

Be brave, thou dearest heart." With ready
    grasp
A bow he seizes, that with other arms
Upon the wall is hung; the arrow fits:
Upon its helpless prey straight speeds the
    shaft;
The tender body fallen to the ground,
Flutters a wounded wing and then is still.
Each to the other looks, but scant the time
For word or look or taking of farewell.
The mighty rock whereon the castle stands
Instant apart is rent, and to the black
Abyss unknown, immeasurable,
Is flung the ancient house and all that folk.
Unuttered woe! From the deep heart of
    earth
A sluggish water pours, and all is told.
Of that so joyous band not one remains.
God rest their souls and give them of his
    peace!

Still stands the cliff, and little clinging vines
Its creviced sides have broidered all with green;
Over its slopes the wild anemone
Wanders in color, and the bracken waves,
And through its feathery grasses sighs the
      wind;
But rare the foot of man, for it is said
That upon All-Souls' Eve when spirits tres-
      passed
Do brief to earth return, upon the height
Its massive front the castle rears anew,
Lights from the windows gleam and music
      floats,
And voices send their carol through the night.
The infrequent traveler checks his steed to
      gaze,
But when he looks again, no castle there,
Only the great rock silvered by the moon;
Nor any sound is in that solitude
Except the sullen plashing of the lake.

WAKE NOT THE GODS.

Wake not the dreadful gods; we say their sleep
  Will last unbroken through the centuries;
  But should we err, assuredly for these
Our halcyon days we shall be made to reap
A bitter harvest.   Over us shall sweep
  The wrath which no oblation may appease,
  Since it mislikes them that their slaves should
     seize
One hour wherein they may forget to weep.

For this, for this the gods are envious,—
  Never for them the unforeseen delight,
    The uncertain rapture which must have an
    end, .
Yet, while it lasts, illumes the world for us,
  The summer lightning of life's stormy night,
    When soul draws nigh to soul, and friend
    meets friend.

BALLADE OF CHARITY.

When gentle dames together sit
  And gossip, as they sometimes will,
I fear that while they sew and knit
  And dainty China tea-cups fill,
  A careless drop or two they spill,
Less soothing than the rare Bohea,
  Nor, while they reputations kill,
Let fall the veil of Charity.

Success succeeds; we worship it;
  The golden calf we follow still.
The man who fails we coldly twit
  With lack of brains and strength and skill,
  And with our mocking glances chill
The heart that aches for sympathy.
  Oh, for a drop from Pity's rill!—
Let fall the veil of Charity.

44

I have, I frankly must admit,
  A liking for poor Tom or Bill,
Who, like myself, get hardly hit,
  In climbing up Life's rugged hill.
  With many a scramble, many a spill,
We trudge along in company,
  Upon our mingled good and ill
Let fall the veil of Charity.

ENVOY.

  Princess, my song hath little wit;
    Of thy divine sweet clemency,
  Upon the words that here are writ
    Let fall the veil of Charity.

THE FAMINE IN RUSSIA.

Ill shall it be in time to come for those
    Who, careless living 'neath a bounteous sky,
    Calmly indifferent, can hear the cry
Of thousands helpless in the mortal throes
Of desolating hunger. If we chose
    What saving ships across the sea should fly
    Climbing th' uneasy wave, each day more
        nigh
To the sad northern land of steppes and snows.

Almighty God! If by a miracle,
    As in old days, thou now shouldst prove thy
        power
        And show the exceeding brightness of thy
            face
So long withdrawn—! With love unspeakable
    Touch thou men's hearts, and but for one
        short hour
        Let mercy all the suffering world embrace.

WESTMINSTER ABBEY.

From these stained windows what a light is
  thrown
 By the descending sun, what tender blues,
 What passionate purples blend their varied
  hues
O'er nave and roof and ancient carven stone!
Now there arises the melodious tone
 Of voices which such harmonies diffuse,
 As in their harpings heavenly seraphs use;
And hark, the organ's supplicating moan!

Seems it not well that through this wondrous
  pile,
 Which guards the ashes of the sons of song,
  Whose souls have fled to stars beyond our
   ken,
Music should echo on from aisle to aisle,
 And evermore its cadences prolong
  Throughout the Mecca of all Englishmen?

47

THE UNATTAINABLE.

Dreaming I stand upon a mountain side;
  Beneath me is a forest, and beyond
  A marshy plain whose every little pond
Shines like a shield, for it is evening-tide.
What farther lies?   Do not these dim woods
    hide
  A faery place?   For when I most despond,
  Faint bells I hear,— or is it but my fond
Vague fancy?—chiming through the forest wide.

What is beyond the shimmering morass?
  I may not know, nor whether gods or men
    Do there inhabit; nor by what strange
      spell
Nightly am I constrained to rise and pass
  To the weird forest, and the phantom fen,
    Only to hear, far off, that pleading bell.

BOOTH IN HAMLET.

Once in Life's rosy dawn I saw the towers
  Of Elsinore rise on the pictured scene;
    The king, the ghost, and the unhappy queen
I saw, and fair Ophelia with her flowers,
And heard the slow bell toll the passing hours;
  But when you entered with dejected mien,
    The others seemed as though they had not
        been;
We wept with Hamlet, for his griefs were ours.

And here, to-night, amid the listening crowd
  That hangs upon your lips, I see the flame—
    The sacred fire nor time nor age can quell,
Howe'er the mortal frame be changed and
        bowed,—
  Burn clear as the high places whence it came.
    Pass on, thou royal Dane; hail and fare-
        well!

BALLADE OF MEMORY.

This night my soul shall liberate
   Itself from brooding mists, and fly
Where the old dreams and fancies wait
   Beneath a magical fair sky.
   Soft, scented breezes, passing by,
Shall lull me into slumber deep,
   And nothing hurtful shall come nigh
To rend my heart, to break my sleep.

One happy dream to compensate
   For grievous years on years!   My cry
May reach the gods, my low estate
   From their bright seats they may descry,
   And send a blessed memory
Which shall have strength afar to keep
   Sad thoughts that come, I know not why,
To rend my heart, to break my sleep.

My soul remains a leaden weight.
  The gods were kinder to deny
Our vain desires than grant too late.
  How cold, with what averted eye
  The past returns; it will not die,—
Its haunting shades about me creep,
  And miserably sob and sigh,
To rend my heart, to break my sleep.

ENVOY.

Princess, be warned, nor tempt thy fate,
  Else shalt thou have full cause to weep,
When ghostly memories pass thy gate,
  To rend thy heart, to break thy sleep.

BALLADE OF THE DARK HOUR.

In happy hours that careless went,
  Through many a bright, unconscious year,
With friends whose smiles new gladness lent
To youth's sweet morning, dew-besprent,
  From skies that seemed as crystal clear,
    No warning shade was thrown
  To prophesy the coming fear
    Of our dark hour alone.

Then sorrow came. On us she bent
  Her look; she drew more near.
At first we knew not what she meant.
"Pass on!" we cried; "you are not sent
  Life's opening buds to sear.
    Pass on to lands unknown!"
  Ah me! she watched the first sad tear
    Of our dark hour alone.

52

Since then she dwells beneath our tent,
  Never to disappear.
She only hears when we lament
Our hidden griefs and hours misspent,
  And lost loves on the bier;
    For she at length has grown
Into our souls to domineer
    O'er our dark hour alone.

ENVOY.

Prince, of the Present make good cheer,
  For you her sway shall own,
Prostrate before her brow austere
  In your dark hour alone.

BALLADE OF DEATH.

That we may live our lives at all,
 The cunning gods have thrown
A curtain heavy as a pall,
And raised a high dividing wall
 Before the land unknown
  Whose bliss none uttereth,
To keep each weary, earthworn thrall
  From the soft arms of death.

And fears that stoutest hearts appall
 Within man's breast are sown.
Life's cup is mingled wine and gall;
He hath his days of festival,
 Which claim him for their own,
  So his foot tarrieth;
He dreads to leave his lighted hall
  For the soft arms of death.

The creatures of a day, we crawl
  Each on the earth alone,
Eager our brother to forestall,
Nor heed the murmur mystical,
  The ceaseless undertone
  Of that low voice which saith:
"Soon shalt thou leave this idle brawl
  For the soft arms of death."

ENVOY.

Friend, when for me the shade shall fall,
  With my last failing breath
My soul to your dear soul shall call
  From the soft arms of death.

MNEMOSYNE.

Queen of the Muses, I have loved thee well.
  Still in thy temple, servile, suppliant,
  Have I besought the shadowy ghosts that
      haunt
Thine inmost shrine, petitioned them to tell
Of the gray past, and all that there befell.
  Now thy mysterious songs no more enchant,
  Thy hoarded wisdom is an idle vaunt.
Have mercy on thy slave—undo the spell!

The dwellers on the far Olympian heights
  Have joy in thee, immortal, calm, content,
    With futile tears their eyes are never wet.
But I remember only lost delights,
  And languish in perpetual banishment
    From all desirèd things.   Let me forget.

A GREETING.

Now in Midwinter, see! the buds unfold;
   The yellow poppies open one by one;
The mountain streams, bound by no despot cold,
   Flash through the woods, rejoicing as they
      run.
A most fair land: it is the land of gold;
   It is the land of pleasure and the sun,
Pacific as the waters round it rolled.
   Come hither, all ye wretched, wronged, fore-
      done!

Here Freedom dwells, and all men worship her.
   Throned in the west, she sendeth from afar
Words of good-will, a radiant messenger
   Of love to all, the holiest avatar.
Peasant and prince, and you, philosopher,
   Sail bravely in across the Golden Bar;
Leave mooning o'er the past and days that were;
   Behold the triumph of the days that are!

THE CHOLERA.

CHANT FUNÈBRE.

Others may fear thee; what care I
   How soon thy stilling hand be laid
Upon this heart?   I shall not sigh
   To be again a shade.
     Upon the shore
Of Acheron I 've friends galore.

But this poor simple earth of ours
   Doth all her uncomplaining best
To keep, with music, light and flowers,
   The young ones in her nest.
     The old, the worn
Be thine—the tares amid the corn.

Majestic pestilence!—be kind;
   Take not the mother from her child,

The youth from her—for love is blind—
  Who late upon him smiled.
    Pass not their way—
They 'll welcome thee some future day.

For here, alas! too many are
  With toil and sorrow quite undone,
Who long to reach a purer star
  Where love and life are one.
    Short is thy shrift:
A moment—and the shadows lift.

TWO SONGS.

I.

If where you dwell, in other lands,
  Your soul and mine should meet,
O, would you take my waiting hands,
  Or pass with hasty feet?

It may be in that purer air
  A clearer sight is given,
And hearts may meet with rapture there,
  That here by fate were riven.

And so, I watch the lagging years
  Go on, in cloud and rain,
For somewhere in those mystic spheres
  We two shall meet again.

II.

Believe not that the ¡dead forget,
　In this most peaceful place;
My heart is heavy with regret
　Because of thy fair face.

Forgive the colder, duller brain
　That could not understand
Thy love, nor to its heights attain
　In that obscurer land.

By the white doors of living light
　I wait, I watch for thee,—
The first to greet thy nearing flight
　Of all this company.

THE ISLE OF SKYE.

The dream returns, I have my wish,
  I see Dunvegan's Hall;
The moon sleeps fair on Grishornish,
  I hear the boatmen call;—
And it's O, for a nook in a broomy dell,
  Where the thyme its balm distils,
And the rich, rare smell of the heather-bell
  That grows on the Highland hills.

What song is that, so quaint and sad?
  Down the gray loch it rings;
The summer days when I was glad
  Before my eyes it brings;
And it's O, for the kindly Northern speech,
  And the simple fisher-folk,
And the tangled reach of the wild sea-beach,
  Where my soul to life awoke.

The South is fair, but not to me;
  Though by the sunlight kissed,
It lacks the nameless witchery
  That wraps the Isle of Mist;
And it's O, when in earth I lie alow,
  By the far Hebridean wave,
May the heather grow, and the west wind blow
  Round a long-forgotten grave.

GUSTAVE DORÉ.

In what gray fields and by what slow, strange
streams
　Dost thou abide, and is thy pencil still
　Busy with phantasies and shapes of ill?
Perchance thou hast forgotten earthly dreams,
And fame to thee a faded vision seems,
　Since of Nepenthe thou hast drunk thy fill,
　And watched the grapes of Proserpine distil
Their juice in some dim vale where faint light
gleams.—

That fabled land by no man visited
　Since wan Eurydice the singer bore
　Nigh to the dreadful gates—upon its shore
Hast thou found rest for weary heart and head?
　Or doth the raven sit above the door?
Is there remembrance with the shadowy dead?

THE VIOLIN.

The Master's fingers from his violin
   Draw forth a melting music, soft and slow;
   Quavers in air the faint adagio;
The scherzo follows with tumultuous din,
As if a thousand elves were hid within
   The fragile shape, whence now arise and grow
   Sounds as of voices tremulous with woe,
Deeply deploring some unearthly sin.

Listening, I hear the secret of thy heart,
   And why thy trembling strings must still
         complain:
     Thou art a lamentation and a cry
Of bodiless souls, that, turning to depart
   From off the threshold of the vast inane,
     Call upon us who are about to die.

CALIFORNIA.

While by their hearths men sat and stories told
  Of fabled islands hidden in the west,
    Or spent their lives, all fruitless, in the quest,
Thou wert asleep upon thy bed of gold,
Thy treasure safely kept within thy hold,
  Until, awaking from a dream of rest,
    Thou baredst the secrets of thy mighty breast,
And all thy wonders to the world unrolled.

And yet, beware! much gold can dull the brain,
  Can clog the springs of fancy, and destroy
    The soul with slow and subtle alchemy,—
A baser race may rise to live for gain,
  Pitiful dullards may thy spoils enjoy,
    And thou, thyself, be but a mockery.

AUTUMN.

I have watched them passing—youth, and love,
    and hope,—
        All are gone from me.
With their ghosts I wander down life's autumn
    slope,
        Silent, drearily.

Where the roses blossomed, splendid, purple,
    red,
        Grows the lotos-tree.
Faded flowers and leafage round my path are
    spread,
        Sad and strange to see.

"Failure, only failure;" all the fancies fine
        Fled as shadows flee:
But the dead are sleeping where the ivies
    twine,
        Oh, so peacefully !

JACKSON'S LAST WORDS.

"Let me pass over the river, and rest in the
shade of the trees."

From Elysian fields they had come; they were
met
Their comrade's last pangs to appease;
Far and fast had they flown, for they could not
forget
The night-watches under the trees.

They whispered, "Commander! the night-watch
is set,
The old banner floats on the breeze;
We are drawn up in line to the youngest cadet,
Under the shade of the trees."

63

He saw them—oh, wonder!—the fever and fret,
  The traces of pain and disease
Were gone, and he cried, "Good my friends
      let me get
    Away to the shade of the trees."

So he passes with them to the white parapet.
  What welcoming voices are these!
Do you think that he grieves, or has any regret,
  Under the shade of the trees?

Mighty hero! the sun of whose glory unset
  Gleams on the limitless seas,
We shall pass o'er the River and walk with you
      yet,
  Under the shade of the trees.

ENCHANTED GROUND.

In all these lands there is no restful place,
    No spot secure from sorrow may be found;
Care lends a shadow to the dearest face,
    And many a heart conceals a mortal wound.
    But far away I know a fairer ground,
A forest where 't is summer all the year;
    Amid its leafy mazes horns resound,—
There Jaques stands musing by the dying
      deer,
And Touchstone fleets the time with jest and
      merry fleer.

There smiling Rosalind, in April charm,
    Torments Orlando with her mirthful mood.
How innocent are all and free from harm!
    What gracious spirits in this solitude!

But I must hie me to another wood,
Outside of Athens, an it be not gone,—
But no, it stands as stately as it stood,
What time Titania flouted Oberon,
And the bewildered lovers slept its sward upon.

What soft enchantment wraps my soul away?
The magic juice hath sure been spilt on me.
Behold the sunken ships within the bay!
Prospero weaves his web of glamourie,—
Imprisoned Ariel struggles to be free,—
Miranda with her Prince talks heart to heart.
This is the isle where I have longed to be,
Most subtly tinted by the Master's art;—
Here let me rest, nor ever from these shores
depart!

IN EXTREMIS.

I.

I spoke, but what I know not;
  I saw, yet did not see:
The heart's deep fountains flow not
  In extreme misery.
I closed the door upon the friend
Whose love had lasted till the end.

All was a blank—all yearning,
  All fear, all hope were gone:
No star in silence burning
  Was ever more alone.
I lent my body to the knife,
And knew that it was death or life.

"Not to give too much trouble,"
  Was the last conscious thought;
Then, like a breaking bubble,
  It passed, and I was naught,
Until, awaking on my bed,
I looked around astonishèd.

II.

An atom in the scale of things
   (Atoms can suffer), quietly
I watch the slow gray light that brings
   Another day of agony.

Before me lies the broad, bright bay;
   I see the lumber-laden ships,
Ready to start upon their way.
   How cool and fresh the water slips

About their prows!   Bon voyage,— I
   Am sailing fast, more fast than you,
To other seas, a stranger sky,
   And shores that mortal never knew.

ROBERT LOUIS STEVENSON.

You made a song—it was a song of Skye—
    Full of the seas, the sun, the summer rain;
To some it seemed a gem of melody,
    But others heard therein a cry of pain
    For the wild hills you might not see again.
For me, it touched the springs which secret
        are
    Fast locked within the dull-remembering
        brain.
I would have thanked you—you were gone
        too far—
Nor in the immense of heaven could I discern
        your star.

Only in dreams, only in dreams for me
    The mountains in their stormy glory rise,

Engirdled by the gray and desolate sea,
   And ever changing with a new surprise.
   For them you pined beneath your southern
      skies;
And I, that dearest earth so long untrod,
   Hopeless must love till patient memory
      dies.
The hills, the purple heather,— O, my God!
Might I but rest my head just once upon that
      sod!

But not for me, as never now for you,
   The burn will fill the glen, the plover whir,
Scattering in sudden flight the morning dew
   From moors made sweet with thyme and
      juniper,
   The dun deer glance behind the forest fir,
The billows waste their fury on the strand—
   Treasured delights of the good years that
      were!

No more in dusky Morven shall I stand,
And watch the brown-sailed fisher-boats come
home to land.

Tranced in the splendor of the tropic sun,
    Soft be your cloudless sleep on Vaea's
    height!
Too few your years with swiftest shuttle spun,
    Yet yours the joy in so brief span to write
    That which shall live even in death's de-
    spite.
And as we upward trail on broken wing,
    We hear your call—a trumpet in the night,
And to some "rag of honor" closer cling,
Counting all other loss a passing, trivial thing.

FORGET ME NOT.

I cannot write you as I would.
    Ah me! the slow words will not come.
And yet, I wish you only good;
    The heart speaks, though the lips are dumb.

To-day I found, unwittingly,
    Bright blooming in a sheltered spot,
This floweret.   Let it speak for me.
    Forget me not.

A REMINISCENCE.

Do you remember how we sat together
   Once, at the closing of a winter day?
The fire was lit, for it was bitter weather,
   And you were sad, and I was none too gay.

And how I asked you, in a careless fashion,
   "Why do you knit your brows, as one in
      pain?"
And you replied, with a swift, sudden passion,
   "Three black thoughts hold possession of
      my brain.

"Three faces rise, as in a dream, before me—
   One, a fair woman's, whom I loved in youth;
She robbed me of a good none can restore me—
   My early faith in purity and truth.

78

"The second face is his—my friend, my brother.
　We swore our comradeship should last for
　　　aye;
But that is past—we hardly know each other
　Now, when we meet upon the common way.

"The third, the dearest face—alas! how sadly
　It looks from eyes heavy with tears unshed!
Reproach me not, poor ghost; I loved thee
　　　madly.
　Cold is my heart with thine among the dead."

I heard in silence.　Not a word of cheering
　Came to my lips, so near, so far apart;
No smile had I to give, no glance endearing,
　For I, too, had a sorrow at my heart.

THE SINGERS.

Delicate as Ariel,
   Swayed by every mood,
Choosing still aloof to dwell
   From the multitude.

Gold to them a feeble thing,
   Hardly worth the pains;
Sorrow but a passing sting,
   While the joy remains,—

The divinest joy of song,
   When the facile pen
Traces thoughts that linger long
   In the souls of men.

Thus they live within the light
   Streaming from above,
And their voices in the night
   Sing of hope and love.

We who read their words of flame
  Can with them behold,
In a glory without name,
  Mysteries untold.

All the world before us lies
  In a golden gleam,
And the gates of Paradise
  Open like a dream.

MEMORIA SACRA.

October winds are murmuring
  Their tremulous adagio;
The sad thoughts that to me they bring,
  Could you but know.

This desolate, autumnal day
  Is still to me a day of woe;
I miss you more than words can say,
  Could you but know.

Could you but know the tears I 've shed
  Since you departed, long ago,
'T would vex you in your quiet bed,
  Could you but know.

MEMORIA SACRA.

When light beams brightly on my path,
    And kindly praises men bestow,
My heart a fearful impulse hath,
    Could you but know.

And when, by wandering stars beguiled,
    All dark and drearily I go,
You would be sorry for your child,
    Could you but know.

A MESSAGE.

I send you here the lofty strain
  Of one whose soul was great,
And hope his discipline of pain
  May never be your fate.

And if, on a not distant day
  Of some fast-closing year,
When the tired hand is cold in clay
  Which leaves this message here,

You take the volume from its shelf,
  To glance it idly through,
And read it softly to yourself,
  I shall be watching you.

A MESSAGE.

Although no face your eye shall see
    Nor any sound be heard,
Although your hour of reverie
    Be broken by no word,

I shall be standing by your chair,
    A silent influence
Of which you may be half aware,
    On my departure thence.

THE YEARS.

The fleeting years, the flying years,
 How much they take away!—
Life's early joys, its smiles and tears,
 Youth's beautiful, brief day.

The bitter years, the barren years,
 A dolorous array;
Hope, like a dim mirage, appears
 Upon their desert gray.

The fatal years, the final years,
 Remorseless, they sweep on;
We hail Death's shadow as it nears,
 Impatient to be gone.

ON THE DEATH OF A CAT.

A pretty, timid, gentle thing,
   Whose claws for me were always sheathed,
   That loved the very air I breathed,
Is surely worth remembering.

Perhaps it is not overwise,
   And yet I grieve that nevermore
   Will it peep out behind the door,
With playful welcome in its eyes.

I know, I know I did my best
   To save it from the coming dark,
   And keep alight life's feeble spark,
But—Death was stronger;—therefore, rest,

Poor little friend; and when I, too,
 Shall lie in the unending sleep,
 May one true heart a vigil keep
For me, as I this night for you.

Helpers of man, that draw the plough,
 Or guard the fold, or purring lie
 On cottage hearths, ye beautify
Our lives far more than we allow.

The man who maims his brother man—
 Before him rises up the law,
 August, with eyes that overawe,
Exact his least defect to scan.

And shall not justice fall on them—
 The brutes endowed with human speech-
 Who break the law of love, and reach
Out cruel hands, which none condemn?—

Who care not for the dumb surprise,
  The anguish of the beast o'erdriven?
  Dear God! from thy high place in heaven,
Dost thou not hear thy children's cries?

For are they not his children, they
  Who serve without a recompense,
  Whose looks are full of eloquence,
Expressing thoughts they may not say?

We give them shelter, fire, and food,
  And, in return, they give us all,
  Obedient to our slightest call,—
Their lives one act of gratitude.

Let us to their deserts be just,
  Who hide no hate with smiling guise;
  No venom in their friendship lies—
They purely love, and greatly trust.

EVENING.

When life is nearly over,
  And chimes the vesper bell,
On face of friend or lover
  With long, long looks we dwell;
For it is hard to part—
  To sunder heart from heart.

When life is nearly over,
  Too late we can discern
Good we could not discover,
  And truths we would not learn,
When pressing on in haste
Across life's mid-day waste.

90

When life is nearly over,
　Our evil passions die;
Faint wings about us hover,
　And voices from on high
Call softly to the soul
That neareth now its goal.

When life at last is over,
　And tolls the funeral knell,
Safe, safe beneath the clover
　We rest, and all is well;
Nor are we loth to go—
　The high God wills it so.

IN THE NIGHT.

Look to the East.   Can you see no light,
  No faintest glimmer of dawn to be?
"'T is the blackest hour of the black midnigh t,
  And our chariot wheels drive heavily."

THE HEAVENLY CITY.

While longing from this empty show
  To flee away and rest,
We lift our eyes, and O, the glow
  Of sunshine in the west!

Fair city, where the rescued dwell,
  To thee our feet would haste;
Might we but hear thy music swell,
  Thy living waters taste!

How greatly rise thy splendid walls
  Beside the shoreless sea!
Within the shelter of thy halls
  What happy folk they be!

A FRAGMENT.

The few who hear thy magic voice
    Forsake life's common ways;
They count thine unimagined joys
    More dear than fame or praise.
Yet keen the air upon thy heights,
Lonely thy rapturous delights.

VALE ATQUE VALE.

For me, I never knew the way
   To gain the crowns of life —
A chance spectator of the fray,
   A watcher of the strife.

And so it is not hard for one
   With naught to lose or win,
To mark the setting of the sun,
   And see the night begin.